Thomas Davies

Some Account of the Life and Writings of Philip Massinger

Thomas Davies

Some Account of the Life and Writings of Philip Massinger

ISBN/EAN: 9783337397142

Printed in Europe, USA, Canada, Australia, Japan

Cover: Foto ©Raphael Reischuk / pixelio.de

More available books at **www.hansebooks.com**

SOME

ACCOUNT

OF THE

LIFE and WRITINGS

OF

PHILIP MASSINGER.

LONDON:

MDCCLXXXIX.

THE
LIFE
OF
PHILIP MASSINGER.

THOUGH *Maffinger's* Claim to an eminent Rank amongft the Englifh Dramatick Writers has never been contefted, and the
Criticks have placed him immediately after
Shakefpeare, B. Jonfon, Beaumont and *Fletcher*;
notwithftanding we have certain Evidence that
his Plays were much applauded in their Reprefentation, and warmly commended by con
temporary Writers, yet fuch has been the
unaccountable Fate of this excellent Author,
that the Name of *Maffinger*, till within thefe
twenty Years, has been funk in Obfcurity,
and almoft buried in Oblivion. None of our
Stage Poets, from the Reftoration to the Beginning of his prefent Majefty's Reign, have
taken the leaft Notice of him or his Writings *.

B   The

---

* In the Year 1751 Propofals were printed for a new
Edition of *Maffinger's* Works with Notes and Obfervations
in

The Silence of *Dryden* is not to be accounted for on any Principle of Reafon or Juftice. But indeed the Man who could treat *Shirley* with fuch Contempt as to rank him with the Dunces of his Macfleckno, might wifh to ftifle the Memory of a Writer, who was as much fuperior to him in Dramatick Excellence, as *Dryden* himfelf was above all other Writers of his Time, in the Vigour, Harmony and Variety of his Numbers.

Mr. *Rowe* has paid *Maffinger* a very great Compliment indeed, but it muft be granted that it is at the Expence of his own Candour and Honefty. In his Tragedy of the *Fair Penitent*, he condefcended to fteal the Plot, Characters, and fometimes the Sentiments of the *Fatal Dowry*. But this Conduct was as weak as it was unfair; for a fmall Acknowledgement of his Obligations to the original Author would not only have faved him from the Difgrace of a fhameful Detection, but have made that a legal Prize which is now an Act of Piracy.

We* are told indeed, that *Rowe* lived in the Days of literary filching; when Plagiarifm was a fafhionable Trick amongft Authors. Such an

in five Volumes 12mo, at the moderate Price of *Two Shillings and Sixpence* per Volume, but the Subfcription went on fo flowly that the Project was dropt.

* It was the Fafhion with the Wits of the laft Age to conceal the Places from whence they took their Hints or their Subjects.

Goldfmith's *Life of Parnell.*

Excufe

Excufe I think ought no more to be admitted in the Courts of *Parnaſſus*, than a Robber's juſtifying his Thefts by the great Number of his Aſſociates and Companions, would be allowed to be a good Plea in *Weſtminſter Hall* or at the *Old Bailey*.

The little that can be known of *Maſſinger*, I have principally gleaned from the ſcanty Materials which *Antony Wood*, in his *Athenæ Oxonienſes*, and Mr. *Langbaine* in his Lives of the Dramatick Poets, have afforded me. That curious and laborious Searcher into Hiſtory, Biography and Antiquities, Mr. *John Oldys*, in his MS. Notes on *Langbaine*'s Poets, has pointed out ſome Miſtakes of both theſe Authors reſpecting *Maſſinger*, and has ſometimes ſuggeſted Matter of Intelligence not unworthy of Notice.—To Mr. *Reed* of *Staples Inn* I am indebted for the frank Communication of theſe MS. Notes, a complete Liſt of the various Editions of *Maſſinger*'s Plays, and ſeveral uſeful Hints relating to him and his Works.

Philip Maſſinger, the Son of * *Philip Maſſinger*, a Servant belonging to the Family of *Pembroke*, was born at *Saliſbury* in the Year 1584. He was entered a Commoner at St.

* I cannot gueſs from what Information *Oldys* in his MS. Notes gives the *Chriſtian* Name of *Arthur* to *Maſſinger*'s Father; nor why he ſhould reproach *Wood* for calling him *Philip*; ſince *Maſſinger* himſelf, in the Dedication of the *Bondman* to the Earl of *Montgomery*, ſays expreſsly that his Father *Philip Maſſinger* lived and died in the Service of the Honourable Houſe of *Pembroke*.

Alban's Hall, *Oxford*, in the feventeenth Year of his Age, in 1601 ; where, though encourage d in his Studies by the Earl of *Pembroke*, yet, fays *Wood*, he applied his Mind more to Poetry and Romances for about. four Years or more than to Logick and Philofophy, which he ought to have done, as he was patronized to that End.

By ftyling *Maffinger's* Father a Servant, *Wood* did not, I fuppofe, intend to convey any Mark of Degradation, or any other Meaning than that he was a Gentleman of the Earl of *Pembroke's* Retinue. It is certain that, in the Year 1597, he was employed by that Nobleman as a Meffenger on no trifling Bufinefs to Queen *Elizabeth*, whofe Charadter would admit of nothing unimportant or infignificant in her Service. Amongft the *Sydney* Papers, publifhed by *Collins*, there is a Letter of *Rowland White*, Efq; to Sir *Robert Sydney*, in which he acquaints him that Mr. *Maffinger* was newly come from the Earl of *Pembroke* with Letters to the Queen for his Lordfhip's Leave of Abfence on St. *George's* Day. This carries a confiderable Proof that the Bearer of Letters to *Elizabeth*, on a Matter perhaps which fhe thought important, was no mean Perfon ; for no Monarch ever exadted from the Nobility in general, and the Officers of State in particular, a more rigid and fcrupulous Compliance to ftated Order than this Princefs.

A different Relation of *Maffinger's* College Education is given by *Langbaine*: He informs us, that *Maffinger's* Father was a Gentleman belonging

longing to the Earl of *Montgomery**, in whose Service, after having lived many Years, he

* *Langbaine* has committed a Mistake respecting the Title of *Montgomery*, which did not belong to the Family of *Pembroke* till the Decease of *William* Earl of *Pembroke*, who died 1630. *Clarendon*, in his Character of *Philip* Earl of *Montgomery*, who was afterwards Patron to *Massinger*, informs us that he was very young when *James* I. came to the Crown ; that he was taken with Lord *Herbert*'s Comliness of Person, and his Skill in Riding and Hunting ; and that after bestowing many Honours upon him, he created him in 1605, Earl of *Montgomery*. But *Clarendon* perhaps did not know the real Cause of Lord *Herbert*'s Advancement. The Behaviour of the *Scots* to the *English* on *James*'s Accession to the Throne of *England* was generally obnoxious and much resented. At a Meeting of *English* and *Scotch* Gentlemen, at a Horse Race near *Croyden*, a sudden Quarrel arose between them, occasioned by one Mr. *Ramsay*'s striking *Philip* Lord *Herbert* in the Face with a Switch. The *English* would have so far resented this Affront, as to have made instantly a national Quarrel of the Matter ; and one Gentleman, Mr. *Pinchbeck*, rode about the Field with a Dagger in his Hand, crying out, ' *Let us break our Fast with them here, and dine with them in London.*' But *Herbert* not resenting this contumacious Behaviour of *Ramsay*, the King was so charmed with his peaceable Disposition, that he made him a Knight, a Baron, a Viscount and an Earl, all in one Day. *Osborne*, from whom I transcribe this, and who lived during these Transactions, intimates, that *Herbert*'s Cowardice prevented not only that Day from being fatal to the *Scots*, but ever after through all *England*. The Mother of *Herbert*, the renowned Countess of *Pembroke*, to whom Sir *Philip Sydney*, her Brother, dedicated his *Arcadia*, tore her Hair when she heard the News of her Son's Dishonour. It is certainly more probable, that King *James* should raise *Herbert* to the Title of Earl for this pacifick Behaviour, which prevented a national Quarrel, than that he should confer that Honour upon him merely for his handsome Face ; more especially as he was never suspected to be a Minion of *James*.

B 3. died ;

died; that he beftowed a liberal Education on his Son, fending him to the Univerfity of Ox-*ford* at the Age of Eighteen, in 1602, where he clofely purfued his Studies in *Alban* Hall for three or four Years.

The Accounts of *Wood* and *Langbaine* are fo contradictory, that it is impoffible to reconcile them. Nor can we, perhaps, decide peremptorily which of thefe Guides we fhould follow. Both were diligent Inveftigators of Truth, and both we fhould imagine to be equally capable of getting fuch Materials as were fufficient to authenticate their Narratives. But, after ferioufly balancing their Merits, I believe the Reader will be inclined to juftify my preferring the Authority of *Wood* to *Langbaine*. The former lived nearer the Times of *Maffinger* than the latter; he was conftantly refident at Oxford, and had the beft Opportunities to know in what Manner the Students then profecuted their Studies. Befides, it was a Practice familiar to our ancient Nobility, to patronize and educate the Children of Gentlemen who formed their Retinue. The illuftrious Houfe of *Pembroke* I believe has ever diftinguifhed itfelf by the Love and Encouragement of the fine Arts; *Shakefpeare*'s and *Beaumont* and *Fletcher*'s Works, and many other Books of Poetry, dedicated to the Family of *Herbert*, give an irrefragable Proof of their generous Difpofition to favour and reward the Followers of the Mufes,

Wood

Wood fays that *Maſſinger* was ſent to *Oxford* in 1601; but according to *Langbaine* he was not there before 1602. This ſeeming Difference may be eaſily reconciled; for the Year then began and ended according to that Mode of Reckoning which took place before the Alteration of the Style by Act of Parliament 1752.

William Earl of *Pembroke* ſucceeded his Father *Henry*, who died *January* 19, 1601.— *Maſſinger* muſt then, agreeably to *Wood*'s Account, have been ſupported at the Univerſity by the Generoſity of this Nobleman. But it ſeems, our Author's Application to the more ſuperficial, though alluring Studies of Poetry and Romances, fruſtrated the Intention of his Patron, and diſqualified him from receiving a Degree; to obtain which, an Application to Logick and Philoſophy was abſolutely neceſſary; as the Candidate for that Honour muſt paſs through an Examination in both before he can obtain it.

A Degree conferred upon a Scholar by an Univerſity is, in our Days, held a diſtinguiſhed Mark of Merit; and in thoſe Times of ſevere Diſcipline and ſtrict Application to Learning, I ſuppoſe it was eſteemed a neceſſary Appendage to him, who was ambitious to riſe either in Church or State; and perhaps it was thought by Perſons of the graver Caſt, a Kind of Diſgrace in a Scholar to quit his College without that Proof of Approbation. This ſame Earl of

Pembroke

Pembroke feems to have exacted that Stamp of Merit from *William Brown*, the Author of *Britannia*'s *Paftorals*, who was educated at *Exeter* College, *Oxford*, much about the fame Time our *Maffinger* refided there. From *Wood* we learn, that *Brown* left the Univerfity before he had taken an Academical Degree, and retired to the *Inner Temple, London:* That he returned feveral Years after, viz. in 1624, to his College with * *Robert Dormer*, his Pupil. On the 25th of *March*, in the fame Year, *Brown* received Permiffion to be actually created M. A. although the Degree was not conferred upon him till the *November* following: After he had left College with his Pupil he was gladly *received into the Family of* William *Earl of* Pembroke, *who had a great Refpect for him, and there he made his Fortune fo well that he purchafed an Eftate* †.

Maffinger ftayed at the Univerfity of *Oxford* three or four Years, and then it feems he fet out for *London*, as if impatient to improve himfelf in the Converfation of the eminent Wits and Poets in that Metropolis: And now commenced the Æra of his Misfortunes, as well as his Fame.—I can find no Trace of the precife Time when he began to write for the Stage. The *Oxford Hiftorian*, I have fo often quoted,

* *Robert Dormer* afterwards Earl of *Carnarvon* ; he married Lady *Sophia Herbert*, Sifter of the Earl of *Pembroke*, and was killed at the Battle of *Nafeby*, fighting for *Charles* the Firft.

† *Wood's Athenæ*, Vol. I.

fays,

says, indeed, that after throwing himself out in short Essays, he ventured to try his Abilities in the writing of Plays : but what these Essays were, whether Interlude, Masque, Song, or any other Entertainment of the Stage, we are left to conjecture. The *Virgin Martyr* was, I believe, one of our Author's first Pieces which he wrote in Conjunction with *Decker*, and is far inferior to any of his other Productions. The Plot and Machinery are very extravagant ; and the Play is disgraced by vulgar Dialogue and vile Obscenity, Faults which cannot fairly be laid to *Massinger*'s Charge, who, though occasionally licentious, is never so offensive and disgusting.

Wood and *Langbaine* agree, that *Massinger*'s Dramatick Pieces were approved ; but whatever might be their Success, he soon experienced the unhappy Consequences of disobliging his Patron the Earl of *Pembroke*. This Nobleman's Character is drawn at large by the copious and eloquent Pen of Lord *Clarendon*; who styles him one of the worthiest and best beloved Men of the Age in which he lived. ' He was a Man, says the noble Historian, who conversed with Persons of the most pregnant Parts and Understanding ; and to such, who needed Support or Encouragement, if fairly recommended, he was very liberal. How comes it to pass, that *Massinger*, who was born in the Family of *Herbert*, and bred at the University of *Oxford*, at the Expence of this amiable Man, should be so totally neglected, as it appears from himself that he really was ?

It

It is moſt probable, that our Author's acting in Oppoſition to the Intention of his Patron, and leaving the Univerſity without his Permiſſion, was the leading Cauſe of that low Dependence and Straitneſs of Circumſtances which he laments ſo paſſionately in almoſt all his Applications to the great Men, whoſe Patronage he ſeems rather to have implored than ſolicited.

It muſt hurt a generous Mind to read the almoſt ſervile Supplications and humiliating Acknowledgements with which moſt of his Dedications abound. In the Epiſtle dedicatory of his excellent Tragedy the Duke of *Milan*, he ' *intreats Lady* Catherine Stanhope *to ſuffer the Examples of more knowing and experienced Writers to plead his Pardon for addreſſing his Play to her, the rather, as his Misfortunes have left him no other Courſe to purſue.*' He frankly acquaints Sir *Robert Wiſeman* * ' *that he had but faintly ſubſiſted if he had not often taſted of his Bounty.* The like Acknowledgement of munificent Favour he makes to Sir *Francis Folianby* +, and Sir *Thomas Bland.* In ſhort, the ſame Language, though ſomewhat varied, runs through the greateſt Part of his Addreſſes to his Patrons. The querulous and petitionary Style is peculiar to *Maſſinger* above all other Writers.

When we read the complimentary Epiſtles of this Author's Cotemporaries, many of whom

---

* Dedication of the Great Duke of *Florence.*
† Dedication of the *Maid of Honour.*

were

were diftinguifhed for Wit and Learning, and
fome of them Perfons of fuperior Rank, abound-
ing with the fulleft Approbation of his Merit,
and extolling the Force and Grandeur of his
Genius, we are at a Lofs to account for fuch
a Man's unhappy Condition and dependent Situation.

What the Profits were which accrued to him
from the Reprefentation of his Plays, cannot
now be afcertained ; That the Dramatic Poets
were entitled to One Third Night's Profits in
the Days of *Elizabeth* and *James* the Firft* I
believe is not generally known, but can be au-
thenticated from a Prologue of *Decker* to one of
his Plays. †

* The Progrefs of Liberality is flow; though after the Reftoration, fome Plays were acted Twenty or Thirty Nights
without Interruption, and particularly *Dryden's Sir Martin
Marr-All*; yet the Poets could not obtain more than the Profits of one Night, till the latter End of the laft Century,
when, upon the great Succefs of a Play of *Southern*, I believe
it was *Oroonoko*, the Author obtained the Favour of two
Nights : But, in Juftice to the Actors, I muft obferve, that
before the Enlarging the Number of Benefits in Favour of
Authors, the Latter received the whole Money taken on their
Benefit Night without any Deduction for Charges ; *Downes*,
in his *Rofcius Anglicanus*, acquaints us, that *Shadwell* received for his Third Night of the *Squire of Alfatia*, 130l ;
which, fays *Downes*, was the greateft Receipt they ever
had at that Houfe, (*Drury Lane*) in fingle Prices. A few
Years after *Oroonoko* was acted, *Rowe*, by the Succefs of
one of his Tragedies, had the Honour to increafe the Poets
Nights to the Number of Three; fince that Time the Liberality of feveral Managers has frequently gone farther
than the ftated Rule, by giving four, and, I believe, fometimes five Nights to very fuccefsful Plays.

† If this be not a good Play the Devil's in it.

It

It is not Praise is fought for n.w, but Pence,
Though drop'd from greafy apron'd Audience ;
Clap'd may he be with Thunder, that plucks Bays
With fuch foul Hands, and with fquint Eyes does gaze
On Pallas' *Shield, not caring though he gains*
A cram'd third Night, what Filth drops from his
brains.

But we know how precarious the Benefit
Nights of Authors often are, even in this liberal
Age, for by a ftrange Perverfenefs of Fortune,
we fee the Boxes lefs frequented, when an Author's Pains and Merit ought to be rewarded,
than at other Times.

Towards the Beginning of the laft Century
the Tafte for Plays became fo univerfal, that
the Number of Theatres, as Mr. *Steevens* affures
me from the MSS. of *Rymer* the Hiftorio-
grapher, amounted to no lefs than twenty
three.*

So many rival Theatres muft have confidera-
bly diminifhed the Profits of them all. And
though fome of them, fuch as the *Black Friars,*
the *Globe,* the *Phœnix,* the Playhoufe in *Salifbury*

---

* Before the Act which limited the Number of Theatres
in 1736, we had in London no lefs than fix regular Theatres—The Playhoufes of *Drury Lane, Covent Garden, Lin-
coln's Inn Fields, the King's Theatre,* the little Theatre in the
Haymarket, and *Goodman's Fields,* were all open at one Time
and exhibited Plays, Operas, &c. befides a Playhoufe in
James Street, called the *Slaughter Houfe,* and another in *Vil-
liers Street, York Buildings;* there was a Third at *Windmill
Hill,* and another at *May Fair;* and in many of the great
Taverns of this Metropolis, particularly the *Devil Tavern,*
Temple Bar, Plays were occafionally acted.

Court,

Court, and the *Cock Pit*, were more efteemed and frequented by the better Sort of People than the others ; yet from the Smallnefs of the Price paid for the beft Seat, which was Half a Crown, we cannot fuppofe, that the Sum Total taken at One of thefe Theatres, upon an Average, amounted to more than about 25 or 30*l*.*

From this Eftimation we may fairly conclude, that it was impoffible for *Maffinger* to acquire a competent Income from the Reprefentation of his Plays. What Prefents his Dedications produced we cannot eafily conjecture; but from the precarious Circumftances of the Poet, it is reafonable to fuppofe that they were rather fcanty than generous. Nor could the Printer afford a large Sum for the Copy of a Play confifting of ten Sheets, which he fold at the Price of Six Pence. This Information I learn from fome Lines of *W. B.* to *Maffinger*, on his *Bondman*.

> 'Tis granted for your Twelve Pence you did fit,
> And fee and hear, and *underftood not yet* ; †
>
> The

---

* From the Diary of *Edward Allen*, a celebrated Actor, who founded a College at *Dulwich*, in the Reign of King *James* the Firft, we find that the whole Amount of Money taken at the Acting of a Play at his own Theatre, called *The Fortune*, was no more than 3*l*. and a few Shillings ; the Diary fays, indeed that the Audience was very flender.

† This feems to be a much valued Compliment which was frequently paid to our old Dramatic Authors. *Beaumont* tells *B. Jonfon* in fome verfes in praife of his *Catiline*, that he was fo deep in fenfe he would not be underftood in three Ages—An unhappy Panegyrick for a Dramatic Writer, whofe worft Fault muft be Obfcurity.

Dr.

The Author in a Chriftian Pity, takes
Care of your Good, and prints it for your Sakes,
That fuch as will but venture *Six Pence more*,
May know what they but faw and heard before.

I am inclined to believe that * *Shakefpeare*,
as a fharing Actor, gained more Money than any
of his brother Poets did by the Profits of their
Plays.

Though *Beaumont* and *Fletcher* were the Sons
of Men dignified in the Church and the Law,
and confequently fuperior to Indigence ; yet I
do not find that they rejected any lucrative Ad-
vantages they could acquire by their Writings.
It was a Cuftom, fays *Langbaine*, with *Fletcher*,
after he had written the three firft Acts of a
Play, to fhew them to the Actors, and make
Terms with them for the whole.

Without any other Refource but his Pen,
and furrounded as he was with many Inconve-
niences, *Maffinger* might indeed be permitted
to complain, that his Misfortunes obliged him
to write for the Stage.

But however mean the Gratifications which
he obtained from his Patrons, and however fmall

.* *Dr. Percy*, in an Appendix to the Firft Volume of his Re-
licks of Ancient Poetry, quotes, from *Green's Groat's Worth
of Wit*, a Paffage which will tend to confirm what I have
conjectured of *Shakefpeare*'s Share as an Actor. A Player is
introduced in this Pamphlet of *Green*, boafting that his
Share in Stage Apparel would not be fold for Two Hun-
dred Pounds.

the Profits were which arofe from the Acting and Printing of his Plays, he was by no means wanting to himfelf; he was not remifs in pur-fuing his Intereft, or flow in making known his Pretenfions. He applied to fuch noble Lords and Ladies as were allied by Birth or Marri-age to the *Pembroke* Family, and laid Claim to their Favour on Account of his Father's Con-nections with that noble Houfe.

The Earl of *Montgomery* being accidentally at the Reprefentation of the *Bondman*, and openly approving it, furnifhed the Author with a fair Pretence to dedicate that Play to his Lordfhip. The Beginning of his Addrefs is remarkable, and we may guefs from it that the Dedicator had made fome fruitlefs Attempts to be introduced to the Earl.

However I could never arrive at the Happinefs to be made known to your Lordfhip, a Defire born with me, to make a Tender of all Duties and Services to the noble Family of the Herberts, *defcended to me as an Inheritance from my dead Father*, Philip Maffinger: *many Years he happily fpent in the Ser-vice of your honourable Houfe, and died a Servant of it.*

This claim to Patronage and Protection is here plainly, though modeftly, infinuated. What Favour he afterwards experienced from this Nobleman during the Life of his Brother *Wil-liam* Earl of *Pembroke*, concerning whom *Maffin-*

ger,

ger always obferves the moft profound Silence, cannot now be known: But when, by the Death of the * latter, the Earl of *Montgomery* acquired the Title and Eftate of *Pembroke*, there is reafon to fuppofe that our Author's uneafy Circumftances were happily relieved, for in a Copy of Verfes written by him on the Death of *Charles* Lord *Herbert*, the Earl's Son, he addreffed him not only as his fingular good Lord, *but his Patron.* He likewife hints in a Prologue to the Play of *The Very Woman*, that he had revived and altered that Piece in *Obedience to the Command of his Patron :*

> By command
> He undertook this Tafk, nor could it ftand
> With his low Fortune, to refufe to do
> What by his Patron he was call'd unto :
> For whofe Delight and yours, we hope with Care
> He hath revived it.

It is not improbable, that the Refentment of the *Herbert* Family to *Maffinger*, which proceeded from the Offence given to *William* Earl of *Pembroke*, and was merely Perfonal, expired with that Nobleman.

That our Author was happy in the Acquaintance of Men diftinguifhed by Superiority of Rank, and efteemed for their Virtues, is unqueftionable. If Dramatic Hiftory + had not

* *William* Earl of *Pembroke*, to the great Regret of the Public, died *April* 10th, 1630.
+ *Langbaine's* Lives of the Poets.

told

told us that he was beloved for his Modefty, Candour, Affability, and other amiable Qualities of the Mind, the Teftimonies of Sir *Afton Cockaine*, Sir *Henry Moore*, Sir *Thomas Jay*, of *Ford*, *May*, *Shirley* and many Others, would have proved lafting and honourable Records of the Goodnefs of his Mind and the Extent of his Genius.

The Epithets of Addrefs conferred on our Author by his Panegyrifts are remarkably affectionate, *beloved*, *much cfteemed*, *dear*, *worthy*, *deferving*, *honour'd, long known and long loved Friend*, convey the Sentiments of *Maffinger*'s Admirers and Friends with an honeft Warmth, worthy of him and the Congratulators.

The general Approbation given by the Public to the Plays which were produced by the united Efforts of *Beaumont* and *Fletcher*, tempted many other Dramatic Writers to follow their Example, and to commence joint Traders in Wit, but not with equal Fortune. Thefe twin Stars of Dramatic Poetry were fo well match'd in Abilities, fo uniform in ftrength of Sentiment, Brilliancy of Fancy, Elegance of Diction, Variety of Character, and Oeconomy of Plot, that the moft critical Reader could not pretend to determine where *Beaumont* began or where *Fletcher* ended.

But the Public might be eafily convinced, that this Mode of uniting different Capacities in the joint Fabrication of a Play, was a hazardous Undertaking, which fuited very few Wri-

C

ters, and indeed scarce any but the great Originals themselves.

The unequal Powers of Genius generally produced an heterogenous Offspring, for in no Part of Composition did the Partners assimilate or harmonize. The whole Work was at best a Piece of tawdry Patchwork, and of as many Colours as the Patriarch's Coat: The Elements of Matter in Chaos were not more dissimilar and discordant than the separate Scenes of these hand-in-hand Writers.*

Quia Corpore in Uno
Frigida pugnabant calidis, humentia siccis,
Mollia cum duris, sine pondere habentia pondus.

I have dwelt the longer upon this awkward and ridiculous Partnership in Wit, because our *Massinger* suffered greatly by the Practice. The mixing his fine Ore with foreign Dross, gave a Credit to his Allies which they did not merit, at the same Time that his own pure Metal was debased below its genuine Standard. In this Censure I do not mean to include *Nathaniel Field*, who assisted our Author in writing his *Fatal Dowry*; the comic Scenes of this Writer cannot easily be separated from *Massinger's*.

We

* I know of but one Comedy written since the Times of *Beaumont* and *Fletcher*, where the Wit, Fancy, and Humour of two Authors unite so happily, that the Texture of the Whole may be supposed to be woven by one Hand: The Reader will easily guess I mean the *Clandestine Marriage*.

We are told indeed that *Maſſinger* joined with *Fletcher* in the Writing of a few Plays.—Happy ſhould we be to diſcover the Dramatick Pieces in which theſe eminent Writers exerted their mutual Talents; for they were almoſt equally matched, and equally capable to earn the Reward of ſuperior Merit. But for this intereſting Fact, we have no other Proof than the vague Teſtimony of Sir *Aſton Cockaine* *, who, in a proſaick Copy of Verſes, addreſſed to the Publiſhers of *Beaumont* and *Fletcher*, calls upon them to point out which Plays thoſe Authors wrote jointly, and which ſeparately, and to diſtinguiſh the Pieces which the united Muſes of *Fletcher* and *Maſſinger* produced. But this was no more than meer Hearſay; for Sir *Aſton*'s Authority was founded, according to *Langbaine*, upon ſomething which he had heard in Converſation from one who was *Fletcher*'s intimate Friend; we cannot therefore rely on the Truth of this Story.

Sir *Aſton Cockaine* was well acquainted with *Maſſinger*, who would, in all probability, have communicated to his Friend, a Circumſtance which was ſo honourable to himſelf.

---

* To Mr. *Humphrey Moſley* and Mr. *Humphrey Robinſon*,
In the large Book of Plays you late did print
In *Beaumont* and in *Fletcher*'s Name; why in't
Did you not Juſtice? Give to each his due?
For *Beaumont* of thoſe many writ but few:
And *Maſſinger* in other few; the main
Being ſweet Iſſues of ſweet *Fletcher*'s Brain.
But how come I (you aſk) ſo much to know?
Fletcher's chief boſom Friend * inform'd me ſo.
    * Mr. *Charles Cotton*, Author of *Virgil Traveſtie.*

We

We can find no Footſteps of any Intimacy or Acquaintaince between *Shakeſpeare* and *Maſſinger*; though the latter ſeems to have much admired the Works of the former, whom he frequently imitated, and ſometimes, indeed, he has little more than tranſcribed him. But *Shakeſpeare* was older than our Poet by twenty Years, and before *Maſſinger* could poſſibly be known to the Publick, the Father of the *Engliſh* Drama enjoyed that happy Affluence, which enabled him to ſpend the greateſt Part of his Time at his beloved *Stratford upon Avon*; from whence he returned occaſionally to the Metropolis, to viſit his old Friends, and to exhibit ſome new Work which his Leiſure in the Country had tempted him to write for the Stage*.

But we cannot ſo eaſily account for *Ben Jonſon*'s Silence reſpecting our Author, who outlived *Jonſon* only two Years. He, who was ſo ready to praiſe or cenſure all who ſubmitted to, or queſtioned his Authority, has not once mentioned the Man, who after *Shakeſpeare*, *Beaumont*, and *Fletcher*, and himſelf, was the moſt diſtinguiſhed Name in Dramatick Poetry.

But this Poet Critick, in Proportion as the Faculties of his Mind decayed, ſeems to have been more urgent in his Claims to ſuperior

---

* That *Shakeſpeare* wrote for the Stage till the Year 1614, two Years before his Death, has been proved by Mr. *Malone* in a very laborious and well eſtabliſhed Account of the ſeveral Æras when his Plays were acted.—Vide laſt Edit. of *Johnſon's Shakeſpeare*, 10 Vol. 8vo.

Merit;

Merit ; and the publick Voice not according with his own, it rendered him more petulant, prefumptuous, and peevifh. He valued himfelf much upon his Tragick Style, which was his worft Species of Compofition. His Difappointment of Succefs in *Sejanus*, did not prevent him from writing his beloved *Cataline*, as I think my Lord *Dorfet* fome where ftyles it. The ill Fate of this Play feems to have hurt his Mind, and damped his Genius. For nothing which he produced afterwards, if we except fome Scenes of an imperfect Piece, called the *Sad Shepherd*, is worth reading. Tradition informs us, that he wrote his *Bartholomew Fair*, to revenge the Infult offered to *Cataline*. But that Comedy does no Honour to his Memory ; nor to that Publick, who could endure fuch Scenes of vile Ribaldry, low Humour, and vulgar Dialogue. Such a Man, ruffled in his Temper, and difgufted with the World, would not temperately bear fo fuccefsful a Rival as *Maffinger*, who, in Dramatick Poetry, was equal to himfelf, and greatly fuperior to his two adopted Heirs, *Randolph* and *Cartwright*.

Jonfon was, beyond all Controverfy, a Man of confiderable Abilities. He was an excellent Scholar, and the firft Writer who taught the Ufe of critical Learning in Dramatic Compofition. His Humour, though confined to Characters of the loweft Clafs, was genuine ; and in the Conduct of his Scenes, he approached nearer to the Simplicity of the Ancients than any Play Wright of his own Times; but his

C 3 Subjects

Subjects were often ill chosen; and though his
Portraits were correctly designed, his Colour-
ing was dry and unpleasant, his Wit was fa-
shionable, and his Satire local.

His Reputation has sunk in Proportion as
Shakespeare has been known and admired. The
unlimited Obedience to his Stage Laws, which
Jonson exacted, not only from the People at
large, but from his contemporary Authors,
whether Inferiors or Equals, was, in his own
Age, often disputed with Warmth, and rejected with Indignation.

Who can forbear smiling at the extravagant
and absurd Commendations bestowed upon this
Man by *Selden, Beaumont, Randolph, Chapman,
Cartwright,* and others, his Admirers and Flat-
terers?

His Son *Randolph* thus approaches his poetical Parent, with the most profound and reve-
rential Awe:

—When my Muse upon obedient Knees
Asks not a Father's Blessing, let her leese
The Fame of her Adoption; 'tis a Curse
I wish her, 'cause I cannot think a worse!

That his other Son, *Cartwright,* should pre-
fer *Jonson* and *Fletcher* to *Shakespeare,* and even
ridicule the Humour of the matchless Bard,
can be attributed to nothing but a bad Taste,
or the grossest Partiality.

'That

That *Maſſinger* ſcorned to bow the Knee to
this ſelf-elected Monarch, may be proved, I
think, from ſome Lines in his Prologue to the
Baſhful Lover.

' Let others, building on their Merit, ſay
Y'are in the wrong, if you move not that way
Which they preſcribe you ; as you were
    bound to learn
Their Maxims, but incapable to diſcern
'Twixt Truth and Falſehood.'

This is the conſtant Language of *Jonſon*, in
his Inductions, Prologues, and Epilogues. He
will not permit the Audience to decide for
themſelves ; he aſſures them that his Play is
good, and they ought to approve it. In the
Epilogue to *Cynthia's Revels*, he ſwears to the
Excellence of his Workmanſhip.

I'll only ſpeak what I have heard him ſay,
By — 'tis good, and if you like't you may.

When the Practice of adopting poetical Off-
ſpring firſt began, may be with more Rea-
dineſs conjectured than aſcertained. *Jonſon*,
who was as much delighted with an implicit
Homage to his Nod of Authority, as ever beau-
·tiful Woman was charmed with the Number
of her Adorers, was, I believe, the Parent of this
whimſical Cuſtom. *Ben* was not a little fond
of the Delights which flow from ſocial Plea-
ſure, and loved the briſk Circulation of the
Glaſs. Some peculiar Rite muſt have followed
the Chriſtening of the poetical Brat, who, it is
likely, paid the Tribute of a ſumptuous Dinner,
and ſome Gallons of Sack, to his Revered Pa-

rent,

rent, for the much defired Bleffing of Adoption. It were to be wifhed, that the Circumftances attending this Parnaffian Ceremony, had been handed down•to us, and fet forth as explicitly as the celebrated *Leges Convivales*, or *Club Laws* of *Jonfon*, hung up in the *Apollo*, at the *Devil Tavern.* *

In Imitation of *Ben*'s Method of creating Heirs of Genius, other Poets claimed an equal Right of raifing up poetical Offfpring : *Chapman* adopted *Nath. Field*, and what may be thought fomewhat furprizing, *Richard Brome*, the Servant and *Amanuenfis* of *Jonfon*, chofe for his Parent, *Decker*, the avowed Antagonift of his Mafter. Let us hear what Father *Decker* fays to his Son *Brome*, in a congratulatory Poem on his *Northern Lafs*.

To my Son *Brome* on his Lafs.
Which then of both fhall I commend ?
Or thee that art my Son and Friend,
Or her by thee begot ?

Maffinger was, I believe, the laft of thefe poetical Parents ; *James Shirley* was the Offfpring of his Choice ; and with Mr. *Dryden*'s Leave, I will be bold to fay, he was not un-

* In the Beginning of the Reign of *Charles* the Firft, or fome Time after, this Society was eftablifhed by *Ben Jonfon*, and all the Members who compofed it were called his Sons; Dr. *Morley*, afterwards Bifhop of *Winchefter*, and many Perfons of Rank and Merit, thought themfelves honoured to be adopted into the Number of thefe jolly Affociates at the *Devil Tavern*.

worthy

worthy to be chosen Succeſſor to a Man of the moſt approved Dramatical Abilities. As I have given the whole Poem, written by the Father to his adopted Heir, in its proper Place, I ſhall only quote here two Lines, which may ſerve to prove *Maſſinger*'s Opinion of his Child's Abilities.

To his Son *James Shirley*, on his *Minerva*, &c.

Thou art my Son, in that my Choice is ſpoke;
Thine, with thy Father's Muſe, ſtrikes equal
  Stroke.

Here we ſee the modeſt Man, on this Occaſion, throwing off his uſual Reſerve, and aſſuming a Dignity conformable to his Merit.

Amongſt the Friends of *Maſſinger*, I muſt not forget to name *Joſeph Taylor*, a very eminent Comedian; who, in a Copy of Verſes, complimented him on the great Succeſs of his *Roman Actor*, a Play in which *Taylor* repreſented the principal Character. In his Addreſs, he ſtyles the Poet his long known and loved Friend, *Philip Maſſinger*.

Goff, in ſome Latin Verſes, which he wrote upon the ſame Play, celebrates the Merit of the Author and the Player.

Ecce *Philipinæ*, celebrata Tragædia, Muſæ,
Quam *Roſeus Britonum Roſcius* egit, adeſt,
Semper fronde ambo vireant Parnaſſide, &c.
Taylor

Taylor reprefented the Part of *Hamlet*, originally; from the Remembrance of whofe Action in that Character, Sir *William Davenant* is faid to have taught *Betterton* to perform Wonders.

Taylor's Name is to be found in the Lift of Actors in *Shakefpeare*'s and *Beaumont* and *Fletcher*'s Plays. After having lived above forty Years the Admiration of the Publick, in a Variety of principal Characters, he was unhappily reduced to a State of Indigence. It was his Misfortune to furvive the profperous Days of the Theatre, which the breaking out of the civil Wars in 1640, caufed to be fhut up till the Reftoration of *Charles* II. a Period of twenty Years. This excellent Actor died very poor, at *Richmond*, in *Surry*, about the Year 1655.

Maffinger did not live to feel the Miferies of that civil Conteft, which deftroyed the Government of this Kingdom, in Church and State ; he was happy in not feeing the Times of Confufion and Tumult, which though they affect all Ranks of Society, are moft unfriendly to the Mufes. Had he furvived, he might, perhaps, have fhared the Fate of *Taylor*; or have been reduced, like his Son *Shirley*, to earn his Livelihood by teaching Grammar*.

Maffinger died in *March* 1640, according to our prefent Mode of reckoning, or 1639 agreea-

* *Shirley* died during the Rage of the great Fire of *London*, in 1666.—The Terror and Fright which he and his Wife fuffered from this dreadful Conflagration, precipitated the Death of both.

ble to that Style which then prevailed. *Wood* and *Langbaine* both agree in the Manner of his Death ; he went to bed in good Health, and was found dead in the Morning, in his own Houfe, on the *Bankfide, Southwark*. The Comedians paid a juft Tribute to their deceafed Friend by attending him to his Grave. He was buried about the Middle of the Church-yard, belonging to St. *Saviour*'s Church, commonly called the *Bull-head* Church-yard.

Sir *Afton Cockaine*, in an Epitaph which I here tranfcribe from his Poems, publifhed in 1659, acquaints us, that *Maffinger* was buried in the fame Grave with *Fletcher*.

An Epitaph on Mr. *John Fletcher*, and Mr. *Philip Maffinger*, who lay both buried in one Grave, in St. *Mary Overy*'s Church, in *South-wark* *.

In the fame Grave was *Fletcher* buried, here
Lies the Stage Poet, *Philip Maffinger* ;
Plays they did write together, were great
    Friends,
And now one Grave includes them in their ends.
So whom on Earth nothing could part, beneath
Here in their Fame they lie, in fpight of Death.

After what has been faid of our Author, by the Editor, in his elegant Preface, and by the judicious Writer of the Effay on our *Englifh*

* The Regifter of that Church, according to *Oldys*, in his MS. Notes on *Langbaine*'s Life, of *Maffinger*, records that he was buried in one of the four Church Yards belonging to the *Bullhead*.

Dramatick

Dramatick Poets, it may be thought superfluous, as well as impertinent in me, to add any Thing farther upon the Subject.

Notwithstanding, I hope I shall be pardoned if I endeavour to point out some Peculiarities which distinguish this Writer from his Contemporaries.

The Plots of *Massinger*, like those of all our old Dramatists, are borrowed from surprizing Tales, and strange Adventures, from wild Romances and entertaining Novels, or from old Chronicles and well known History. In the conducting of his Fable, he is consistently and invariably attentive.

It is not his Custom, in Imitation of *Beaumont* and *Fletcher*, to write two or three Acts of a Play with uncommon Energy, and after exciting Expectation, and promising Delight, to disappoint the Reader, by unpardonable Neglect, or an utter Desertion of the Fable. I will not pretend to say, that these valuable Authors are always and equally deficient in working up the Catastrophes of their Plays; but I will appeal to their most partial Readers, if they are not often shamefully forgetful and indolent, where the Union of Genius and Judgment is most required *.

* I have either read or been informed that it was generally Mr. *Fletcher*'s Practice, after he had finished three Acts of a Play, to shew them to the Actors; and after they had agreed upon Terms, he huddled up the two last without that proper Care which which was requisite.
                                        Langbaine's Poets, p. 144.

In

In *Maffinger*, Nature and Art are fo happily connected, that the one never feems to counteract the other, and in whatever Rank he may be placed by the Criticks, yet this Praife cannot be refufed him, that his Genius operates equally in every Part of his Compofition ; for the Powers of his Mind are impartially diffufed through his whole Performance ; no Part is purpofely degraded to Infipidity, to make another more fplendid and magnificent ; one Act of a Play is not impoverifhed to enrich another. All the Members of the Piece are cultivated and difpofed as Plot, Situation, and Character require.

The Editor very juftly obferves, that *Maffinger* excels *Shakefpeare* himfelf in an eafy conftant flow of harmonious Language ; nor fhould it be forgotten, that the Current of his Style is never interrupted by harfh, and obfcure Phrafeology, or overloaded with figurative Expreffion. Nor does he indulge in the wanton and licentious Ufe of mixed Modes in Speech ; he is never at a Lofs for proper Words to cloath his Ideas. And it muft be faid of him with Truth, that if he does not always rife to *Shakefpeare*'s Vigour of Sentiment, or Ardor of Expreffion, neither does he fink like him into mean Quibble, and low Conceit.

There is a Difcrimination in the Characters of *Maffinger*, by which they are varied as diftinctly as thofe of *Shakefpeare*. The Hero, the Statefman, the Villain, the Fop, the Coward, the Man of Humour, and the Gentleman, fpeak
a Lan-

a Language appropriated to their feveral Per-
fonages.

Sometimes he takes Pleafure in fmoothing
the Features of a Villain, and concealing his
real Character, till his Wickednefs breaks out
into Action; nor is this Peculiarity in our Author effected by any conftrained or abrupt Conduct, but ftrictly conformable to Dramatick
Truth, and the Oeconomy of his Fable. *Francifco*, in the *Duke of Milan*, affumes, during the
firft Act, fuch a Face of Honefty and Fidelity,
that the Reader muft be furprized, though not
fhocked at the Change of his Behaviour in the
fecond Act. The Villains of *Maffinger* are not
Monfters of Vice, who fin merely from the
Delight they feel in the Practice of Wickednefs.
Francifco, like Dr. *Young*'s *Zanga*, *, carries his
Refentment beyond the Limits of his Provo-
cation ; but a Sifter difhonoured, is, by an *Ita-
lian*, fuppofed to be a fufficient Caufe for pur-
fuing the deepeft Revenge. So *Montreville*, in
the unnatural Combat, fmothers his Rage for
the Injuries he had received from *Malefort*, with
whom he lives in great Familiarity, and the
higheft feeming Warmth of Friendfhip, till he
gains an Opportunity, towards the Clofe of the
Play, to glut his Appetite of Revenge, by ra-
vifhing *Malefort*'s Daughter, and upbraiding
him at the fame Time with the Wrongs which
he had fuffered from him.

* In the Tragedy of the *Revenge*, *Francifco* has fome
Features not unlike thofe of the *Moor*. And I cannot help
thinking, that *Young* had read the *Duke of Milan*, and borrowed a few Hints from that Tragedy.

Maffinger,

Maffinger is equally fkilful in producing Co-
mick and Tragick Delight; his Characters in
both Styles are ftamped by the Hand of Nature. *Eubulus*, in the *Picture*, is as true a Por-
trait of honeft Freedom, fhrewd Obfervation,
and fingular Humour, as *Shakefpeare's Ænobar-
bus*, in *Antony and Cleopatra*. *Durazzo*, in the
Guardian, is inferior to no Character of agreea-
able Singularity in any Author. Joyous in Si-
tuations of the utmoft Peril, he is an impartial
Lover of Valour, in Friend or Foe; he par-
dons the Follies of Youth, by a generous Re-
collection of his own. *Durazzo* forgives every
Thing but Cowardice of Spirit and Meannefs
of Behaviour; a more animated and picturefque
Defcription of Field Sports than that given by
Durazzo is not to be found in any Author.
Maffinger does not ufe the Agency of Fools,
who in *Shakefpeare's* Management produce fuch
admirable Scenes of Delight; *Graculo* and *Hi-
lario* in the *Duke of Milan* and the *Picture* feem
to partake fomething of the *Spanifh Graciofo* and
the *Englifh* Clown; and are employed by our
Author as Choruffes to conduct his Plots.

That *Maffinger* was no mean Scholar every
Reader of Tafte will difcern; his Knowledge in
Mythology, and Hiftory antient and modern,
appears to have been extenfive; nor was he a
mere Smatterer in Logic, and Philofophy,
though *Wood* informs us that he did not apply
himfelf to the Study of thefe Sciences when he
was at the Univerfity. That he was very con-
verfant with the *Greek* and *Roman* Claffics, his
frequent

frequent Allufions to poetical Fable, and his
interweaving fome of the choiceft Sentiments
of the beft antient Writers in his Plays, fuffi-
ciently demonftrate. What he borrowed from
the Claffics he paid back with Intereft, for he
dignified their Sentiments by giving them a
new Luftre; while *Jonfon*, the fuperftitious Ido-
later of the Antients, deforms his Style by
affected Phrafeology and verbal Tranflation;
his Knowledge was unaccompanied by true
Judgment and Elegance of Tafte, and in the
Incorporation of foreign Sentiments with his
own, he underftood not the Means to enrich
his Compofition by artfully borrowing from
the dead Languages.

It was a Fault common to our old Dramatic
Writers, in defcribing the Manners of different Nations, to forget what Painters call the
Coftume; if they laid their Plots in *France*,
Spain, *Italy*, *Germany*, or *Turkey*, the Characters
were merely *Englifh*, and the Cuftoms, Fa-
fhions, Follies, and Vices of our great Metropolis were fure to be introduced, though the
Poet had laid his Scene in *Rome* or *Conftantinople*.

This Incongruity in national Manners runs
through *Shakefpeare*, *B. Jonfon*, and *Beaumont*
and *Fletcher*, as well as *Maffinger*. But though,
in the Conduct of the Drama, this was a great
Impropriety, the Public, I believe, fuffered no
Injury from it. The reigning Enormities and
fafhionable Follies of the Times, were cenfured,
perhaps, with greater Freedom, when the Scene
was

was laid at *Venice*, than if it had been placed in *London*.

Although the Dramatic Poet is the most pleasing, he is at the same Time the most pungent Moralist, and a more powerful Reformer of Vice and Folly than the profest Satirist himself. What are the solemn Sermons of *Seneca*, the laughing Reproofs of *Horace* and the grave Declamations of *Juvenal*, when compared with the deep Reflections of the melancholy *Cardenes*,* and the poignant Strictures of a mad *Timon* or a distracted *Lear* ? *Seneca* dazzles the Reason, *Horace* amuses the Fancy, *Juvenal* alarms the Passions, but *Shakespeare* and *Massinger* warm and refine the Heart.

Massinger, though inferior in pointed Satire to *Shakespeare*, seizes every Opportunity to crush rising Folly, and repel incroaching Vice.

When this Author lived, Luxury in Eating and Finery in Dress universally prevailed, to the most enormous Excess.—These Perversions of natural Appetite and decent Custom he combated with an uncommon Ardor of Resentment, and applied to them the Force of Ridicule wherever he fairly met them. In his *City Madam* he attacks the Pride, Extravagance, and Affectation of the Citizens and their Wives ; he fixes the Boundaries between the gay Splendors of a Court, and the sober Customs of the City. The Ci-

* A Character in the Play of the *Very Woman*.

tizens

tizens, by an awkward Imitation of Court Gaïeties have always rendered themfelves Ridiculous. But this is not all—In abandoning their own primitive Way of Living, they have loft that Influence which can only be preferved by Induftry, Wealth, Oeconomy, Simplicity, and Plainnefs of Manners.

Maffinger does not, like *Shakefpeare* and *Jonfon*, fport with Cowardice and Effeminacy; he confiders them not only as Defects of Character but as Stains of Immorality: *Romont*'s Reproof to *Noval*, a Coward and a Fop, is fingular and bitter.

　　　　　As if thou e'er wert angry
But with thy Taylor, and yet that poor Shred
Can bring more to the making up of a Man
Then can be hoped from thee—Thou art his
　　　　Creature,
And did he not each Morn create thee,
Thou'dft ftink and be forgotten.——I'll not
　　　change
One Syllable more with thee, until thou bring
Some Teftimony under good Men's Hands
Thou art a *Chriftian*. I fufpect thee ftrongly,
And will be fatisfied.
　　　　　　　　　　Fatal Dowry, Act II.

　　But, befides the occafional Cenfure which *Maffinger* paffed upon the growing Vices of the Times in which he lived he aimed at higher Game. He boldy attacked the Faults of Minifters and of Kings themfelves. He
　　　　　　　　　　　　　　　　pointed

pointed his Arrows againſt *Carr* and *Buckingham*, againſt *James* and *Charles* the Firſt.

The puſilanimous Temper of *James* expoſed him to the Scorn of all Europe, and rendered him contemptible in the Eyes of his own Subjects. The warlike Spirit of the Nation was ſubdued by the Cowardice of the Prince. He was called upon by the Voice of his People, and by his Parliament, to aſſiſt his Son-in-Law, *Frederick*, the *Elector Palatine*, and King of *Bohemia*, againſt the Emperor *Ferdinand*, who deprived him at laſt of the beſt Part of his Dominions. *James*, inſtead of furniſhing Troops to *Frederick*, contented himſelf with ſending Ambaſſadors to the *Auſtrian* Court, the Futility of which Conduct was ridiculed upon the Stage at *Bruſſells*.

Maſſinger, though from the general Tenor of his Writings, he appears to have been a firm Friend of Monarchy, and warmly attached to Government in Church and State, was not a Favourer of Arbitrary Power, or inclined to put an implicit Faith in the Word of Kings; he was averſe from embracing the Doctrines of Paſſive Obedience and Non-Reſiſtance *, ſo much

---

* The Conduct of *B.* and *Fletcher* ſo far as it reſpects the Duty which Subjects owe to Kings, deſerves Notice : They preach up the moſt unreſerved Submiſſion to Princes, and zealouſly maintain

    The Right Divine of Kings to govern Wrong.

Yet they make no Scruple of plotting againſt, and deſtroying tyrannical Princes.

                Vide The Maid's Tragedy.

incul-

inculcated by *James*, in his Speeches to Parliament, and his Court Divines in their Sermons. *Maffinger* was a good Subject, but not like other Poets, his Contemporaries, a flavifh Flatterer of Power, and an Abettor of defpotick Principles.

Our Poet, in his Play of the *Maid of Honour*, under the Characters of *Roberto*, King of *Sicily*, and *Fulgentio* his Favourite, undoubtedly drew the Portraits of *James* and his Minion, *Carr* or *Buckingham*, or perhaps both.

The Duke of *Urbino*, by his Ambaffador, craves the Affiftance of the King of *Sicily*.— *Roberto* pleads in his Refufal, the Injuftice of the Duke's Caufe.—*James* too, would not own the Title of his Son-in-Law to *Bohemia*, though he was chofen by the free Votes of the Eftates of that Kingdom ; nor would he permit him to receive the Honours due to his high Rank, from pretended Scruples of Confcience or Motives of Honour. *Bertoldo*, from many fpirited Arguments, urges the King to grant the Duke the requefted Aid. The following Speech will, I believe, confirm my Conjecture of the *Sicilian* Prince's Refemblance to our *Britifh* Monarch.

——May you live long
* *The King of Peace*; fo you deny not us
The Glory of the War ; let not our Nerves

* *Rex Pacificus* was a Title that *James* affected, and was highly pleafed with.

Shrink

Shrink up with Sloth, nor for Want of Em-
    ployment
Make younger Brothers Thieves : 'Tis their
    Sword, Sir,
Muſt ſow and reap their Harveſt. If Examples
May move you more than Arguments, *look on
    England,*
The Empreſs of the European Iſles,
Unto whom alone ours yields Precedence :
When did ſhe flouriſh ſo as when ſhe was
The Miſtreſs of the Ocean? Her Navies
Putting a Girdle round about the World.
When the Iberian *quak'd, her Worthies nam'd;*
And the fair Fleur de Lis grew pale ſet by
The Red Roſe and the White? Let not our Armour
Hung up, or our unrigg'd Armada make us
Ridiculous to the late poor Snakes, our Neighbours,
Warm'd in our Boſoms ; and to whom again
We may be terrible; while we ſpend our Hours
Without Variety, confin'd to Drink,
Dice, Cards, or Whores.

    When this animated Speech was firſt deliver-
ed by the Actor, I cannot doubt but that it was
heard by the Audience with Rapture, and univerſally applauded. The Poet ſpoke the genuine
Senſe of the Nation. *James,* unhappily for himſelf and his Poſterity, inſtead of giving free Li-
berty to the generous Spirit of his Subjects, and
indulging the favourite Paſſion of the Nation
in the briſk Proſecution of a foreign War, by
which he might have gained their Love and
ſecured their Allegiance, cheriſhed the Cockle
of Diſcontent and Sedition, which broke out

with

with Violence in the Reign of his Succeſſor, and caufed the Ruin of the King and Kingdom.

Of *Fulgentio*, King *Roberto*'s Favourite, *Bertoldo* ſpeaks with the utmoſt Contempt:

. ——Let him keep his Smiles
For his State Catamite.

Though *James* was ſuppofed to be averfe from the Fair Sex, and was unfufpeded of any Intrigue with Women, yet he was extremely folicitous to gratify the amorous Paſſions of his two great Favourites, *Somerſet* and *Buckingham.* To forward the former's Marriage with the Counteſs of *Eſſex*, he undertook to prove the Neceſſity of a Divorce between her and the Earl her Huſband, *propter frigiditatem.* Many learned Arguments did he make, and ſeveral obfcene Expreſſions did he ufe, in the Profecution of this unkingly Buſinefs. But if we may credit Sir *Edward Peyton, James* carried his Complaifance to his Minion *Buckingham* ſtill farther, even to a ſhameful Degree of Pandarifm.

" The King entertained Sir *John Crofts* and his Daughter, a beautiful Lafs, at *Newmarket,* that *Buckingham* might have the eaſier Means to vitiate her. And one Mrs. *Dorothy Gawdry* being a rare Creature, the King carried *Buckingham* to *Culford,* that he might have his Will of her : But Sir *Nicholas Bacon*'s Sons and *Peyton* himfelf, contrived to fecure the Lady from the King and *Buckingham*'s bafe Intentions *."

* *Peyton*'s divine Cataſtrophe of the *Stuarts.*

In the fame Play of the *Maid of Honour*, King *Roberto*, willing to fecond the Paffions of his favourite *Fulgentio*, employs his Influence to forward his Match with *Camiola*. For that Purpofe, he fends her a Ring by the Minion himfelf; but the Lady treats *Fulgentio* with that proper Contempt which his Character deferves :

Camiola. Excufe me, Sir, if I
Deliver Reafons, why upon no Terms
I'll marry you.
Fulgentio. Come, your wife Reafons.
Cam. Such as they are, pray you take them:
Firft, I am doubtful whether you are a Man ;
Since for a Shape, trim'd up in Lady's Dreffing,
You might pafs for a Woman*. Now I love
To deal on Certainties; and for the Fairnefs
Of your Compleition, which you think will take me,
The Colour I muft tell you in a Man,
Is weak and faint.
—Then as you are a Courtier,
A graced one too, *I fear you have been too forward.*
And fo much for your Perfon. Rich you are,
Dev'lifh rich, as 'tis reported, and furely have
The Aids of Satan's little Fiends to get it :
And what is got upon his Back, muft be
Spent, you know where.

---

* I have feen *Somerfet* and *Buckingham* labour to refemble Ladies in the Effeminacy of their Dreffings; though in whorifh Looks and wanton Geftures, they exceeded any Part of Womankind, my Converfation did cope withall.
Ofborne's Memoirs of James I.

But

But *Maſſinger* did not confine his Cenſure to perſonal Defects or Vices in the Prince and his Miniſters. He extended his Satire to an open Attack upon Mal-adminiſtration, and the Abuſes of Government.

The Admirers of the two firſt *Stuarts, Charles* and *James,* will confeſs, that though they affected to deſpiſe, yet they greatly dreaded, and cordially hated Parliaments ; Aſſemblies that were obnoxious to them, becauſe they endeavoured to fix proper Bounds to their Power, and inquired rigorouſly into national Grievances. During their Reigns, Patents, Monopolies, Loans, and Benevolences, were the Abuſes univerſally exclaimed againſt. All theſe raged in full Force, when the Dread of a Houſe of Commons was withdrawn.

In the *Emperor of the Eaſt,* a Play acted by the Command of *Charles* I. *Maſſinger* vindicates the Cauſe of the Nation againſt unjuſt and exorbitant Impoſitions, and the Exceſſes of regal and miniſterial Authority. A Scene between the Projectors and *Pulcheria,* the Guardian of the Kingdom, in whoſe Character I think he intended a Compliment to the Memory of Queen *Elizabeth,* gave the Author an Opportunity to ſpeak the public Senſe upon the Stage :

Pulcheria. Projector, I treat firſt
Of you and your Diſciples ; you roar out,
All is the King's ; *his Will's above his Laws,*
And that fit Tributes are too gentle Yokes

For

For his poor Subjects; whifpering in his Ear,
If they would have his Fear, no Man fhould
   dare
To bring a Sallad from his Country Garden
Without the paying Gabel; kill a Hen
Without Excife; or if he defire
To have his Children or his Servants wear
Their Heads upon their Shoulders, you affirm
In Policy, 'tis fit the Owner fhould
Pay for them by the Poll; *or if the Prince*
Want a certain Sum, he may command a City
Impoffibilities; *and for Nonperformance,*
Compel it to fubmit to any Fine
His Officers fhall impofe, &c.

The Reader of public Tranfactions, during
the whole Reign of *James*, and the greateft Part
of *Charles* I. will acknowledge the Juftice of
Maffinger's Cenfure. I fhall only obferve, that
the City of *London* was frequently the Object of
courtly Impofition and arbitrary Taxation.—
From the Authority of *Camden*, in his An-
nals of *James* I. we learn, that that Monarch, in the Year 1620, demanded of the
City of *London* Twenty Thoufand Pounds.
As there was no legal Pretence for the Tax,
the Citizens did not entirely comply with
the royal Mandate; but willingly, as the fame
Author affures us, gave the King Ten Thoufand Pounds. But enough on this Subject.

In a peculiar Strain of Eloquence, and moft
pathetick Art of Perfuafion, *Maffinger* equals,
if not excells, all Dramatick Writers, ancient
                and

and modern; whether he undertakes the De-
fence of injured Virtue, avenges the Wrongs
of suffering Beauty, or pleads the Cause of
insulted Merit; would he sooth, by gentle Insi-
nuation, or prevail by Strength of Argument,
and the Irradiations of Truth!—Does he ar-
raign, supplicate, reproach, threaten or con-
demn!——He is equally powerful, victorious
and triumphant. What are all the laboured
Defences of the Stage, when compared to *Pa-
ris*'s eloquent Vindication of scenical Exhibition
before the *Roman* Senate, in the Tragedy of the
Roman Actor? Would the Reader feel the Effects of filial Piety, in its most amiable and en-
thusiastick Excess, let him read *Charolois* plead-
ing in Behalf of his dead Father, and claiming
a Right to his Body, by giving up his own in
Exchange, in the *Fatal Dowry*. The same
Charolois, justifying himself from the Charge of
Cruelty, in putting to Death an adulterous
Wife, exhibits a still stronger Proof of that
inimitable Art, which our Author so perfectly
enjoyed, to move the Passions, by an irresistible
Stream of eloquent and pathetick Language.

Massinger is the avowed Champion of the
Fair Sex. He lived at a Time when the Spirit
of Chivalry, which owed its Institution to the
Honours due to the beautiful Part of the Crea-
tion, was not quite extinguished. And however
the Excesses of Knight Errantry may be ridiculed, there is something noble in the Idea of pro-
tecting Beauty in Distress, and rescuing female
Innocence from Oppression. Our Author always
rises above himself, when he describes Beauty
                                        and

and its Effects. When a fine Woman is the Subject, his Verses run with a sweet Fervour, and pleasing Rapidity; like *Milton*, when ruminating on the divine Verses of *Homer* and other sublime Poets, *Maſſinger*'s Ideas when feeding on his favourite Subject.—

Voluntary move
Harmonious Numbers.

The Females of *Beaumont* and *Fletcher* are for the moſt Part violent in their Paſſions, capricious in their Manners, licentious, and even indecent in their Language.

Maſſinger's Fair Ones are caſt in a very different Mold; they partake juſt ſo much of the male Virtues, Conſtancy and Courage, as to render their feminine Qualities more amiable and attractive.

Four of our Author's Plays are profeſſedly written in Honour of the Fair Sex. The *Bondman*, the *Baſhful Lover*, the *Picture*, and the *Maid of Honour*, are ſo many beautiful Wreaths, compoſed of the choiceſt poetical Flowers, and offered on the Shrine of Beauty.

I have been tempted by my Veneration for this admirable Writer, to go greater Lengths than I intended, in the Inveſtigation of his peculiar Excellencies. *Maſſinger*, the more he is read will certainly be more eſteemed and approved, for no Author will better bear the ſtricteſt Examination; the enjoying the Beauties of this Writer will be attended, perhaps, with ſome little Mur-

Murmuring and Self-upbraiding ; Surprize will be accompanied with Indignation, and Delight with Regret; moft Readers will lament the having had fuch a noble Treafure within their Reach, without having once looked upon its Luftre; and in Proportion as their Negligence has been, will be the Profufion of their Praife and Admiration !

Though it muft be granted, that *Maffinger*, in Compliance with the Times in which he lived, and in Conformity to the Practice of contemporary Writers, did occafionally produce low Characters, and write Scenes of licentious and reprehenfible Dialogue ; yet we muft remember to his Honour, that he never fports with Religion by prophane Rants or idle Jefting; nor does he once infult the Clergy, by petulant Witticifm or Common-place Abufe.